## ABOUT THE BANK STREET READY-TO-READ SERIES

Seventy years of educational research and innovative teaching have given the Bank Street College of Education the reputation as America's most trusted name in early childhood education.

Because no two children are exactly alike in their development, we have designed the *Bank Street Ready-to-Read* series in three levels to accommodate the individual stages of reading readiness of children ages four through eight.

- ○ *Level 1:* GETTING READY TO READ—read-alouds for children who are taking their first steps toward reading.
- ● *Level 2:* READING TOGETHER—for children who are just beginning to read by themselves but may need a little help.
- ○ *Level 3:* I CAN READ IT MYSELF—for children who can read independently.

Our three levels make it easy to select the books most appropriate for a child's development and enable him or her to grow with the series step by step. The *Bank Street Ready-to-Read* books also overlap and reinforce each other, further encouraging the reading process.

We feel that making reading fun and enjoyable is the single most important thing that you can do to help children become good readers. And we hope you'll be a part of Bank Street's long tradition of learning through sharing.

The Bank Street College of Education

D0125812

*For William Robert Davies*
*— W.H.H.*


*For Alexander*
*— P.M.*

For a free color catalog describing Gareth Stevens' list of high-quality books and multimedia programs, call 1-800-542-2595 (USA) or 1-800-461-9120 (Canada). Gareth Stevens Publishing's Fax: (414) 225-0377.
See our catalog, too, on the World Wide Web: http://gsinc.com

Library of Congress Cataloging-in-Publication Data

Hooks, William H.
    Mr. Monster / by William H. Hooks; illustrated by Paul Meisel.
      p.   cm. -- (Bank Street ready-to-read)
    Summary:  Eli's brother comes up with a great scheme to rid their room of Eli's many toy monsters, but then the plan backfires.
    ISBN 0-8368-1774-5 (lib. bdg.)
    [1. Brothers--Fiction.   2. Monsters--Fiction.]   I. Meisel, Paul, ill.   II. Title.
    III. Series.
    PZ7.H7664Mip   1998
    [E]--dc21                                                97-47542

This edition first published in 1998 by
**Gareth Stevens Publishing**
1555 North RiverCenter Drive, Suite 201
Milwaukee, Wisconsin  53212  USA

Printed in Mexico

1 2 3 4 5 6 7 8 9 02 01 00 99 98

Bank Street Ready-to-Read™

# Mr. Monster

by William H. Hooks
Illustrated by Paul Meisel

Gareth Stevens Publishing
**MILWAUKEE**

4

# Mr. Monster

My brother Eli is five years old
and really loves monsters.
Everyone gives him monsters—
   for his birthday,
   for Christmas,
   for Halloween—
because they think Eli's monster phase
is so cute.

5

Eli will only eat cereal
that has monsters hidden
inside the box.

I used to call him Mr. Bubble Gum.
Then I began calling him Mr. Monster
to tease him.
But it didn't work.
He loves the name Mr. Monster!

Mr. Monster and I share a room.
I should say, I share a room
with Eli and his monsters.
They are all over the place.

8

There's a big, green plastic one
standing in the corner.
There's a whole zoo of little monsters
on the chest.
Stuffed monsters cover Eli's bed
and lie around on the rug,
trying to see who can look the ugliest.
Thank goodness I have the top bunk—
the only monster-free spot in the room.

I've just about had it with monsters.

It was time to call my friend Roberta.
I knew she'd help come up with a plot
to clear the monsters out of the house.

# The Plot

Roberta looked around the room.
"Yuck!" she said.
"This looks like the bad guys took over."
"Listen, Roberta," I said.
"You've got to help me get rid
of these monsters."
"No problem," said Roberta.
"Where's the nearest trash can?"
"Not funny, Roberta. Come on,
let's put our thinking caps on."
Roberta scratched her head.

"Tell Eli the monsters don't like being
out where there's light," she said.
"That's it?" I asked.
"That's all there is to it," she said,
rolling her eyes as though
I was some dummy for asking.

"It'll never work," I said.
"Eli will pull down the shades
and never put on the light.
Then we'll have a dark room
that's still full of monsters."

Suddenly Roberta's idea
gave *me* an idea.
"I'll tell Eli there's a gobble monster
hanging around."
"What's a gobble monster?"
asked Roberta.
"One that gobbles up other monsters,"
I told her. "I'll tell Eli he'd better hide
his monsters in a dark closet,
where they'll be safe."

Roberta and I shook hands.
"Consider your room monster-free,"
she said.

18

# The Plot Works

Eli and I were sitting on the front stoop.
"Hey, Mr. Monster," I said to him,
"I saw a gobble monster peeking
in our window last night."
Eli's eyes grew big.

"I don't have a gobble monster," said Eli.
"I don't think you want one," I told him.
"I want every monster in the world."
"Not the gobble monster," I said.
"What kind of monster was it?" he asked.
"One that gobbles up other monsters."
Eli looked puzzled.
"It was a big, purple fuzzy one," I said.
"With sharp claws and long fangs."
Eli twisted his mouth to one side.
He does that when he's worried.
"I think you'd better hide your monsters
in the closet," I said.

Eli jumped up
and ran into the house.
I followed him.
He ran to our room.
I peeked in.

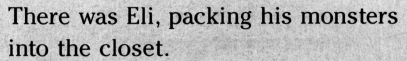

There was Eli, packing his monsters
into the closet.
I watched, just outside the door,
until he'd stuffed them all in.
The last to go was the big, green one.

But when he pushed the end of its tail
inside and slammed the door—
*POP!*—the door flew open,
and the green monster bounced out.
Eli caught it on the first bounce.
Then he stuffed it under the bed.

What a beautiful room!
Not a monster in sight.
"It's working, Roberta,"
I whispered.

# The Plot Backfires

It took Eli a long time to get
to bed that night.
First he checked the monsters
in the closet.
Then he crawled under his bed
to check on the big, green monster.

28

I was almost asleep when I heard him
dragging a chair over to the closet.
I sat up.
Eli pushed the chair
against the closet door.
"Hey, Mr. Monster," I said, "settle down!"
"Got to make sure my monsters
are safe," he said.
He sounded a little scared.

I don't know how long I'd been asleep
when I felt someone tapping me.
It was Eli, halfway up the bunk ladder.

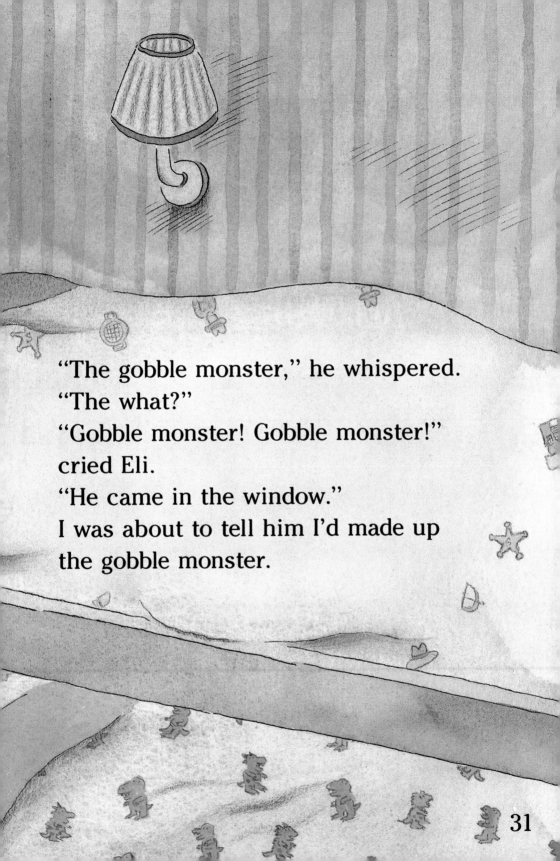

"The gobble monster," he whispered.
"The what?"
"Gobble monster! Gobble monster!"
cried Eli.
"He came in the window."
I was about to tell him I'd made up
the gobble monster.

Instead I asked, "Where is he?"
"Under the bed, gobbling up
my green monster!"
I turned on the light and jumped down.
I reached under the bed
and pulled out the green monster.
"Not a bite out of this monster," I said.
"He was here. I heard him," said Eli.

*BANG!*
There was a loud noise
outside the window.
"That's the gobble monster!" cried Eli.
I ran to the window.
Outside I saw two stray dogs.
"It was only dogs in the trash," I said.
"It was the gobble monster," said Eli.
"There's no gobble monster.
I made it up," I told him.
"Now go back to bed."

Eli didn't believe me.
He was up and down all night.
Neither of us got any sleep.
The next morning I called Roberta.
"How are the monsters?" she asked.
"Our plot just backfired!" I told her.

# The Scare Nook

Every night Eli claimed
he heard the gobble monster
somewhere in our room.
It did no good to tell him
I'd made it up.
Was I sorry I'd ever told him about
gobble monsters!
I even stopped calling him Mr. Monster.

That weekend Roberta and I were
playing catch.
I was missing a lot of balls.
"What are you thinking about?"
she asked.
"How to get rid of a gobble monster,"
I said.

"You need a scare nook," she said.
"What's a scare nook?" I asked her.
"Oh, just a little thing to scare off gobble monsters," Roberta said.
"Where can you buy one?"
"You can't buy them," she answered.
"Well, how do you get one?"
"You have to make it. Come on," she said.
"You're no good at catch today, anyway. Let's go make a scare nook."

On the way to Roberta's house
she told me about scare nooks.
"You make a little monster
out of an old sock or mitten."
"Then what?" I asked.

"Then you give it to Eli.
You tell him that the scare nook
will keep the gobble monster away."
"Roberta," I shouted, "you are the
smartest person I know!"

We spent the afternoon
making a scare nook.
Roberta gave me a pair of red socks.
"Hey, with two socks we can have
a two-headed scare nook," I said.
"Great," said Roberta. "There's no way
a gobble monster can sneak up on you
with a two-headed scare nook!"

We made pop eyes on the scare nook
with Ping-Pong balls.
We put on really ratty hair made
from a worn-out mop.
Then we painted mouths on both heads,
with tongues sticking out.
"This is turning out to be
a fine scare nook," said Roberta.
I agreed.

That night I tied the scare nook
to Eli's bedpost.
"What's that thing?" he asked.
"A present from Roberta and me."
"I don't want any more monsters,"
he said.
"It's not a monster. It's a scare nook—
to keep gobble monsters away," I said.
Eli looked doubtful.
"As long as we have that scare nook,
no gobble monster will dare come
near us," I told him.

Eli didn't say anything.
He climbed into bed.
I turned out the light.
"You sure?" he asked.
"Sure, I'm sure," I told him.
"Okay," said Eli.

45

From that night on,
Eli lost interest in monsters.
But I have to talk
to Roberta again—
now he's into scare nooks!

47

William H. Hooks is the author of many books for children, including the highly-acclaimed *Moss Gown* and, most recently, *The Three Little Pigs and the Fox.* He is also the Director of Publications at Bank Street College. As part of Bank Street's Media Group, he has been closely involved with such projects as the well-known Bank Street Readers and Discoveries: An Individualized Reading Program. Mr. Hooks lives with three cats in a Greenwich Village brownstone in New York City.

Paul Meisel attended Wesleyan University and the Yale School of Art. He is the illustrator of *Mr. Bubble Gum,* the first book about Eli and his older brother, *And That's What Happened to Little Lucy,* and *Monkey-Monkey's Trick.* Mr. Meisel lives in Connecticut with his wife and two children.